This book belongs to:

....

....

For Sophie and Hannah,
with love ~ JP

For V, the perfect
design partner ~ CP

Editor: Tasha Percy
Designer: Verity Clark
Editorial Director: Victoria Garrard
Art Director: Laura Roberts-Jensen

Copyright © QED Publishing 2015

First published in the UK in 2015 by QED Publishing
A Quarto Group company, The Old Brewery, 6 Blundell Street, London, N7 9BH

www.qed-publishing.co.uk

A catalogue record for this book is available from the British Library.

ISBN 978 1 78493 087 5

Printed in China

The Perfect Job for an Elephant

Jodie Parachini

Illustrated by
Caroline Pedler

QED Publishing

Elsie the Elephant wanted to find a job,
so she went to her mum to ask for help.

"Is there anything you enjoy doing?" Mum asked kindly.

"Um . . ." Elsie thought for a moment and flapped her ears. "Eating?"

"Well, that's a start. How about being a chef?" said Mum.

So Elsie went to Zebra's Snack Shack.
She tried her very best to mix and stir
and bake just like the other chefs.

They made
lumpy cakes,

drizzle
drinks

and **gorgeous
goodies.**

Everything looked
so delicious that
Elsie couldn't
help herself . . .

She ate **everything** in sight!

"Get out!"
cried the other chefs.

"This is no job
for an elephant!"

Elsie moped her way back home.

Elsie's mum nuzzled her
and said, "Let's see . . .

. . . you're great at trumpeting.
Why don't you become a musician?"

So Elsie joined Parakeet's Piccolo Band. The birds were making lovely **tweets** and **toots.**

Elsie raised her trunk and gave a **loud . . .**

"TARRRUUMP!"

"Ohh! Too loud!
This is no job for
an elephant!"
complained the birds.

A sad Elsie once
again returned home.

"Hmm," said Mum. "Maybe you should use your creative skills."

"I do like making things," said Elsie.

"Splendid! Maybe you'd like to be an artist," said Mum.

She sent Elsie to Flamingo's Pottery Studio.

Inside, Flamingo was spinning beautiful
pots and bowls on his wheel.

"That looks like fun," thought Elsie.

She started shaping . . .

. . . and patting . . .

. . . and spinning
the clay until . . .

. . . uh-oh!

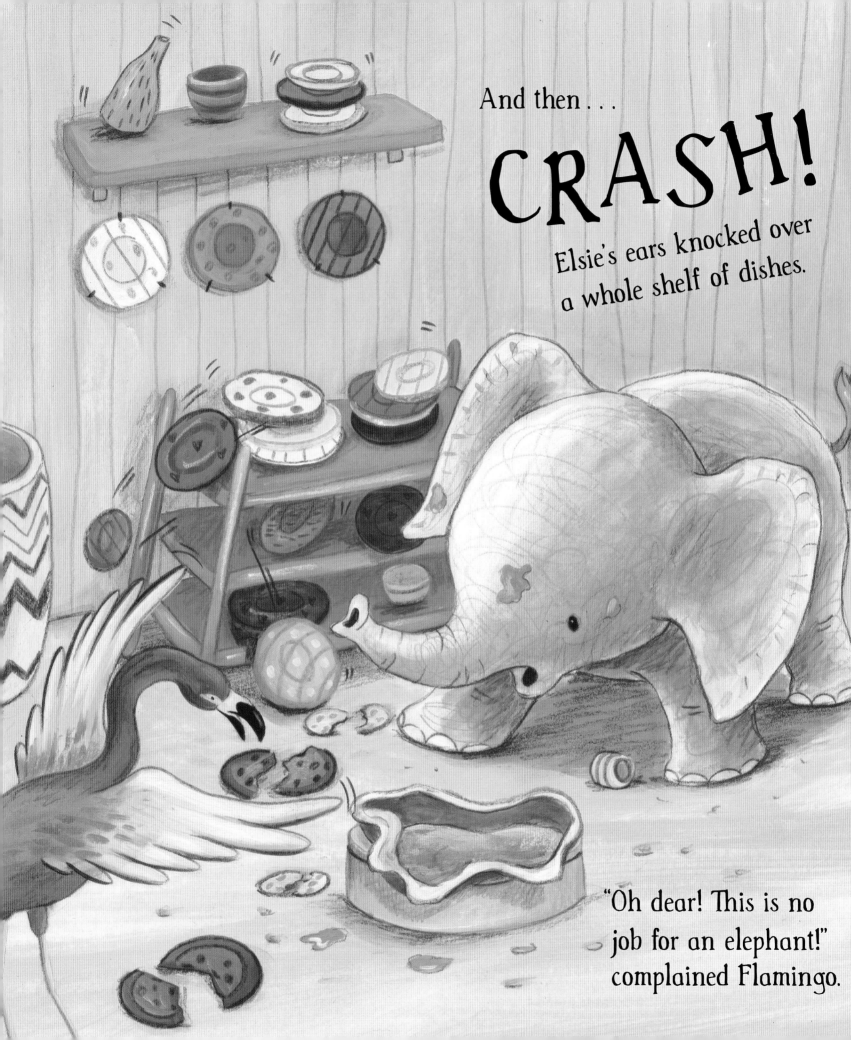

And then . . .

CRASH!

Elsie's ears knocked over a whole shelf of dishes.

"Oh dear! This is no job for an elephant!" complained Flamingo.

At home, Elsie began to cry. "I eat too much,
I'm too loud and I'm clumsy.
I'll never be good at
anything," she wept.

"Nonsense!" said Mum. "Let's think. You're also strong,
your trunk is powerful and you like helping people.

I'm sure there's a job that's perfect
for you somewhere . . ."

Suddenly they heard
a terrible wail.

"Help!"

Zebra's Snack Shack had caught on fire!

Animals were running this way and that.

No one knew what to do.

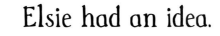

Elsie had an idea.

She ran as fast as she could
down to the watering hole.

She sucked up the
water with her trunk...

...and sprayed the
Snack Shack.

"Elsie, you did it!" cried the grateful animals.
Elsie grinned.

She was a
FIREFIGHTER!

Everyone agreed, it really was
the perfect job for an elephant.

Next Steps

- Can the children think of other jobs an elephant would be good at? What do they think would be the perfect job for a monkey? How about a giraffe?

- What do the children want to be when they grow up and why? Is there more than one job that they would like to do?

- Ask the children if they have jobs or responsibilities that they have to do around the home – like tidying their room or setting the table. Are there jobs that they prefer doing? Why?

- Some jobs take skills that need to be studied or learned whereas others take concentration, talent, patience or creativity. What skills would it take to be a chef? How about an athlete, a doctor, a firefighter, an artist or an astronaut?

- How do the children feel when a task is too difficult for them? Do they give up or do they keep trying? Do they think Elsie could become a good chef, musician or artist?

- Being a teacher is a difficult job. Do you think Zebra, Parakeet or Flamingo were good teachers? How should they have helped Elsie?